Crispin
and the
3 Little Piglets

Hello! My name is

Cheezy Mouse™

I want to be your friend
Please luv me

WARNING: The name **CHEEZY MOUSE**™ and the heart-shaped ID badge
are protected by the trademark and copyright act of 1988.
Removal of this ID badge and renaming this toy
will destroy its market value
and render it
WORTHLESS

A Doubleday Book for Young Readers

Published by
Random House Children's Books
a division of
Random House, Inc.
1540 Broadway
New York, New York 10036

DOUBLEDAY and the anchor with dolphin colophon
are registered trademarks of Random House, Inc.

First American edition 2003
First published in Great Britain by Doubleday,
an imprint of Random House Children's Books

Visit us on the Web! www.randomhouse.com/kids
Educators and librarians, for a variety of teaching tools, visit us at
www.randomhouse.com/teachers

Cataloging-in-Publication Data is available from the Library of Congress.

ISBN: 0-385-74633-4   0-385-90859-8 (lib. bdg.)
The text of this book is set in 20-point Two Can Bodoni Infant.
Manufactured in Singapore
March 2003
10 9 8 7 6 5 4 3 2 1

Crispin
and the 3 Little Piglets

cyber psnail

KARAOKE KID Sing-a-long Sound System

Good Vibrations
Oscillating Slumber Sling
ASSEMBLED IN AFGHANISTAN
UNDER STRICT UN SUPERVISION

Swan Lake Scented Nappy Disposal System

Lil-Bo-Peep CCTV Monitor

homeopathic ultrasound suspension babybather

sterila

3

Ted Dewan

A DOUBLEDAY BOOK FOR YOUNG READERS

To the triplets,
Patrick, Kyle, and Matthew

This little paper house
is for you guys

Crispin Tamworth was a pig who had it all to himself.

He had loads
of stuff to
play with

and two
best friends,
Penny and Nick.

One day, Mrs. Tamworth said to Crispin, "How would you like a little brother or sister?"

"Why would I want one of those?" asked Crispin.

"Oh, you'll like it when the time comes," grunted Mr. Tamworth.

But Crispin
wasn't sure
he wanted
a new piglet.

His friend
Penny had
little brothers
and sisters.
So Crispin went
over to Penny's
house to see what
it might
be like when
the time came.

There were an awful lot of them,
but it looked like fun.

After he left
Penny's house,
Crispin thought
it might be nice
to have a
little brother
or sister
to play with.

After all, there
would only be
one of them.

Finally the time came. Mrs. Peck, the housekeeper, took Crispin to the hospital where Mr. and Mrs. Tamworth were staying.

"Look, Crispin," said Mrs. Tamworth. "Aren't they sweet?"

Three little piglets were wriggling in their blankets.

The first piglet
made a mess
all over
Crispin's shirt.

The second
piglet just
screamed and
screamed.

But the third
piglet was quiet
and cuddly.
"I'll take this one,"
said Crispin.

Crispin was very surprised when all three little piglets came back to his house.

Next day, Aunt and Uncle Potbelly came over with a great big CHEEZY MOUSE™ for Crispin.

Then they hurried away to play with the piglets.

Paula from next door came over with a great big CHEEZY MOUSE™ for Crispin.

But then she nipped away to play with the piglets.

Finally, Nick's dad came over with a great big CHEEZY MOUSE™ for Crispin.

But even *Nick's dad* slipped away to play with the piglets.

It just wasn't fair.

When the 3 Little Piglets made a great big mess, everybody said, "Aren't they cute?"

LITTLE PIGS! LITTLE PIGS! LET ME COME IN! NOT BY THE HAIR ON MY CHINNY CHIN CHIN!

So Crispin made a great big mess and said, "Look! I'm a little piglet, too!"

He was sent outside.

It just
wasn't
fair.

When the 3 Little Piglets
screamed and cried,
everybody said,
"Ooo, the poor dears,"
and played their favorite song!

THEN I'LL HUFF AND I'LL PUFF AND
I'LL BLOW YOUR HOUSE DOWN

But when Crispin
screamed and cried,
saying, "Help me! I'm a
little piglet, too,
and I want
a different song!"

he was sent outside.

One day, when the piglets were listening to their Big Bad Wolf song for the hundredth time, Mrs. Tamworth said,

"Oh, Crispin, I'm so busy and tired . . . won't you *please* keep the 3 Little Piglets quiet for a while?"

So Crispin tried
to keep the
3 Little Piglets
quiet for
a while.

But soon
there was
trouble,

and
crying,

and he was sent outside.

The next day, Nick came over.

"I hate the 3 Little Piglets,"
grumbled Crispin. "I hate their
stupid Big Bad Wolf song."

"Crispin's afraid of
the Big Bad Wolf . . .
tra la la!" sang Nick.

"No, I'm not!"
shouted Crispin.
"*I'm* the BIG BAD WOLF!
And I'll huff . . . and I'll puff . . .

and I'll *BLOW*
your house down!"
roared Crispin.

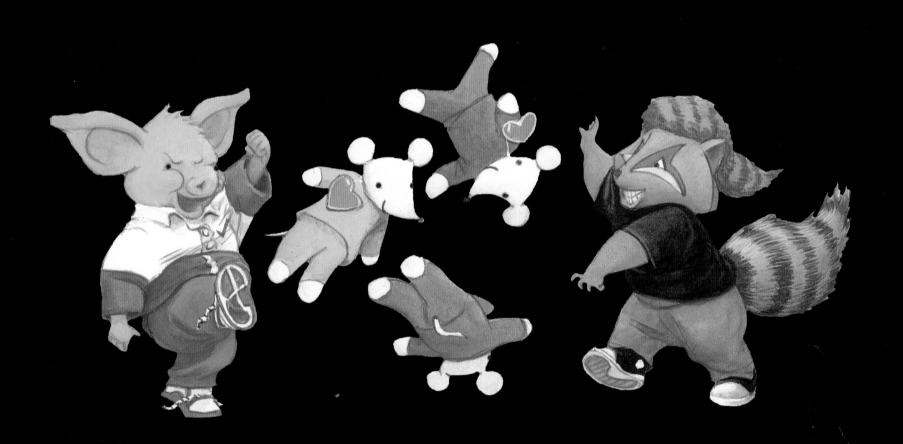

BIG BAD WOLF
became Crispin's
favorite game.

Crispin, Nick, and Penny were busy playing BIG BAD WOLF one day when Mrs. Peck said, "These piglets keep getting under my feet. Won't you kids let them play with you?"

"Aw, they're too little to play BIG BAD WOLF," Crispin whined. "They'll just cry."

But Penny knew a few good games they could all play . . .
like **RACING FAST CARS.**

And EMERGENCY HOSPITAL.

And the 3 Little Piglets
didn't cry all afternoon.

But then Nick and Penny went home,
and Crispin didn't know
what to do.

ANTRUM
TENT

bloc

stage
3B+

He rubbed the hair
on his chinny chin chin.

Then he said,
"You want to hear your stupid
Big Bad Wolf song?"

Yes

Yes

Yes

So they all climbed up on the sofa.

And they huffed, and
they puffed, and . . .

Things got a little
out of control.

Big Bad Wolf
and the
3 Little Piglets
were sent to
their rooms.

LITTLE
PIGS
KEEP
OUT

But Big Bad Wolf crept out
and knocked on the door of
the 3 Little Piglets, whispering,

"LITTLE PIGS! LITTLE PIGS! LET ME COME IN. . . ."

and he read them
their favorite
story.